The dot com Leprechaun

written & illustrated by Caroline Stellings

BREAKWATER

Library and Archives Canada Cataloguing in Publication

Stellings, Caroline, 1961-
The dot com leprechaun / written & illustrated by Caroline Stellings.
ISBN 978-1-55081-328-9
I. Title.
PS8587.T4448D68 2010   jC813'.6   C2010-901036-1

© 2010 Caroline Stellings

ALL RIGHTS RESERVED. No part of this publication may be reproduced, stored in a retrieval system or transmitted, in any form or by any means, without the prior written consent of the publisher or a licence from The Canadian Copyright Licensing Agency (Access Copyright). For an Access Copyright licence, visit www.accesscopyright.ca or call toll free to 1-800-893-5777.

BREAKWATER BOOKS LTD. acknowledges the support of the Canada Council for the Arts which last year invested $1.3 million in the arts in Newfoundland. We acknowledge the financial support of the Government of Canada through the Book Publishing Industry Development Program for our publishing activities. We acknowledge the financial support of the Government of Newfoundland and Labrador through the department of Tourism, Culture and Recreation for our publishing activities.

Printed in Canada

For Breakwater Books, who published my first book.

Lucy looked out the window of her frame house on the Bonavista Peninsula and watched the evening mist roll in from the sea. Bursts of white spray splashed the rock-bound coast.

"This is the most beautiful place in the world," she thought.

But times were tough in the area, and her family had been hard hit. They weren't able to make the payments on their home and had to leave by the end of summer. Lucy couldn't imagine what life would be like without the sound of the waves, or the sight of puffins, warming themselves in the sun.

She went to her desk and turned on the computer. It was an old computer that didn't do much, but Lucy needed a distraction – anything to keep her mind off leaving Newfoundland.

It was always slow to start, but this time it lit up in an instant! A brilliant green light filled the screen and made a strange noise.

"Oh no," she said. "My computer's breaking down."

"It is not!" shouted a voice from inside the monitor. "Stop fiddling with that mouse. And whatever you do, *don't touch the delete key!*"

Lucy watched with amazement as a tiny man came into focus.

"A leprechaun!" she said.

"Yes, a leprechaun – and I need help!"

"How can I help you?" asked Lucy.

"It's a long story and I haven't much time left, so let's just say I've been ensorcelled."

"Ensorcelled?"

"Ensorcelled," insisted the leprechaun. "Sent to the Internet by that silly witch Elfrida. All because the shoes I made didn't fit her big feet. They're even silver satin! But she put the spell on me and here I am, stuck in the web," he explained.

"You mean forever?" Lucy inquired.

"At moonrise tonight, Elfrida is going to give the supreme curse and I will become a cyber-leprechaun."

"That's not long from now!"

"I know," he replied briskly. "Why do you think I've come for help? I'm desperate!" He threw both arms into the air. "If only I could find Angora."

"Angora?"

"Elfrida's cousin. The two of them are always trying to get the better of each other. Maybe she could …" He stopped. "But there's no time. You're my only hope."

"I still don't understand what I can do." She gazed into the monitor. "What's your name, anyway?"

"Caboto."

Lucy put her hand over her mouth to cover a smile.

"It beats Rumpelstiltskin!" snapped the leprechaun. "I come from a long line of Cabotos. My ancestors came here with the Great Admiral himself – John Cabot – in 1497."

"So you've always lived in Bonavista," she asked, "but where?"

"In your root cellar."

"That creepy cellar? It hasn't been opened in a hundred years!" Lucy exclaimed.

"I like it. No one bothers me there. But I'll never see my home again if you don't help me."

"What do I have to do?"

The leprechaun explained that in the root cellar, in his home behind a self-bored stone, were the silver shoes he'd made for the witch. Lucy was to reach inside, pull them out and take them to the fairies' midsummer night dance, before Elfrida recited the final words. "If they fit, the spell will be broken."

"I can't do it," cried Lucy. "I can't go into that root cellar." She shuddered. "It's full of old webs and who knows what?"

"How'd you like to be caught in this web? If you don't help me – and soon – the fairies will begin their dance and Elfrida will say the incantation, and I'll–"

Lucy clicked off the monitor and fled from her room. There was no way she could do what Caboto asked. She couldn't go inside the cellar.

Not then.

Not ever.

She slammed the screen door and ran out to the edge of the cliff. The waves crashed beneath her, and for a moment, Lucy forgot the leprechaun and the root cellar, and thought instead about having to leave Bonavista. She wondered why it had to happen to her.

"There is nothing worse than being forced out of your home," she said. "Nothing."

As Lucy looked down at the rugged Atlantic shoreline, an alarming thought struck her. "I can't let it happen to Caboto!"

She dashed back to her room and switched on the computer.

Nothing happened.

She tried again, but the leprechaun was gone.

"Caboto? Caboto, can you hear me?" called Lucy. "I want to help you. Tell me how to find the self-bored stone."

The screen lit up and the leprechaun reappeared.

"It's too late. I'm finished."

Lucy clenched her fists. "No, I can do it."

"Well, you'll have to hurry," he said. "The stone is on the back wall of the cellar. Pull it loose and inside you'll find the silver shoes. When the fairies dance around the thorn tree, convince Elfrida to try them on." He paused for a moment. "But don't let anyone follow you to the dance, or the fairies will disappear."

"Won't I scare them off?" she asked.

"Not if you carry the silver shoes," replied Caboto. "And remember, you must never tell anyone about me, or the fairy-folk, or the self-bored stone."

Lucy grabbed a flashlight and made her way into the yard. She slid down the grassy knoll that led to the root cellar and stood before its craggy entrance. She tugged on the door, but it was warped. Again she pulled, her hands trembling. Then it gave suddenly, swinging outward on a squeaky hinge.

As she stepped inside the musty cellar, a piece of rock fell from the low ceiling and dropped onto the back of her neck, sending a chill up her spine. Lucy took a deep breath. "It's only gravel," she reasoned, while crossing the dirt floor cautiously.

She inched along the back wall until her light revealed the special stone. "There it is!" whispered Lucy. She pulled it out slowly and peered inside.

Behind the wall was the most enchanting home she had ever seen. As the moon began to rise, soft light came through the curtains, revealing a cozy fireplace, handmade furniture, tiny tools – and the silver satin shoes! Lucy picked them up carefully and pulled them through the hole. Before putting the stone back, she took one last look at the leprechaun's house. Would he ever make it back?

Time was running out. Lucy rushed through the door and over the hill to the thorn tree. The music had started! There were fairies, elves, pixies and gnomes – and Elfrida, reading from a huge book of spells.

"Bubbling cauldron, C-D ROM,
Find the dot com leprechaun.
Figwort, pennywort, pinch of rue;
Seven drops of Mountain Dew.
Now he'll never sew a—"

"Stop!" yelled Lucy. "Please, stop!"

"Who are you and what do you want?" demanded the witch.

"I am here to give you these. Caboto made them especially for you." She held out the shoes in both hands.

"Ha! That fool! Some cobbler he is. I'll never wear another one of his creations – they pinch my toes."

"Won't you just try on these lovely satin shoes?" pleaded Lucy.

"No."

"But they'd look wonderful with that dress you're wearing." Lucy placed them at the witch's feet.

"No. They'll pinch." The witch refused to try on the shoes.

Then Lucy had an idea.

"Well, if you'd rather not keep them, I could give them to your cousin Angora. I'm sure she'd love them."

"Angora!" exclaimed the witch. She looked down at the shoes. "No, I'll take them. I do wear a lot of silver."

She slid the satin shoes onto her feet.

"I don't believe it," she said. "They're a perfect fit."

"I could have told you that!" declared Caboto, landing with a thud. "Maybe next time you'll listen to me," he shouted over his shoulder, as he ran to join the circle.

Once the dance had ended and the fairies returned to their homes in the hillsides, Lucy heard the foghorn sound in the distance. "How lucky they are," she thought, "to be able to live by the sea forever." As she turned to go back to the house, she noticed something glistening in the grass.

It was a large golden ring.

Lucy held it under the moonlight and read the inscription:

Giovanni Caboto, A.D. 1497.

She stared in astonishment. "This was John Cabot's ring!"

"Now you won't have to leave your home, either," said the leprechaun, as he darted off in a streak of emerald green. "But not a word to anyone about us … not a word."

John Cabot

The Great Admiral, whose Italian name was Giovanni Caboto, was born in the middle of the fifteenth century, probably near Naples. As a merchant trading in spices with the ports of the eastern Mediterranean, Cabot became an expert mariner, and by 1490 moved his wife and sons to Spain so that he could play a role in expanding the frontier of exploration. Monarchs of the day were determined to find new routes to Asia, and the Portuguese and Spanish led the way.

When these leaders turned him down, Cabot moved to England, to the busy port of Bristol and convinced King Henry VII to send him across the mighty Atlantic. His first attempt, in 1496, was a failure, but he succeeded the following year. In the name of the English Crown, he sailed his ship *The Matthew* first to Ireland, and then westward out to sea.

Although the exact location of Cabot's landfall has been debated by historians, most believe that he came ashore on the Cape of Bonavista in June of 1497.

The Root Cellars of Elliston

With its 135 cellars, Elliston, located on Newfoundland's Bonavista Peninsula, is the "Root Cellar Capital of the World." In the days before refrigerators, root cellars were needed to keep food cool in the summer and for the storage of vegetables, preserves and other foods in the winter.

Most of the older cellars in the area were built into the sides of hills with outer walls of rock and wooden roofs covered with sod. It is believed that the first settlers to Elliston (formerly Bird Island Cove) came from the West Country of England and Ireland and brought with them not only the knowledge of how to construct root cellars, but also the tales of leprechauns living in them. You can see the cellars of Elliston on the Internet at www.rootcellars.com.

About the Author
Caroline Stellings

Caroline Stellings is an author and illustrator of children's books from Waterdown, Ontario. She is a professional artist who loves to paint the many birds and animals that inhabit the wetland area near her studio. Her first book was *Skippers at Cape Spear* (Breakwater). This was followed by *Skippers Save the Stone* and the *Malagawatch Mice* series (CBU Press) and a novel, *The Contest* (Second Story Press).